nardurna.

Thames & Hudson Australia wishes to acknowledge that Aboriginal and Torres Strait Islander people are the first storytellers of this nation and the Traditional Custodians of the land on which we live and work. We acknowledge their continuing culture and pay respect to Elders past and present. We gratefully acknowledge the Gudanji/Wakaja people and Ryhia Dank. Thank you for sharing your story.

nardurna.

A FIRST NATIONS COLOURING BOOK

by Ryhia Dank

HELLO,

My name is Ryhia Dank. I am a Gudanji/Wakaja woman sharing my stories through art. Drawing from my upbringing in a remote Indigenous community in the Northern Territory, I've created this colouring book. It invites individuals from all backgrounds to connect with my art and discover the beauty of Gudanji/Wakaja storywork. Embark on a meaningful journey of exploration and embrace the transformative power of art as we celebrate our shared experiences and create connections.

CONNECTIONS

Connections is about families.

This artwork is about my three family groups, Gudanji, Wakaja and Kalkatungu. The largest circle represents Gudanji and the middle circle is Wakaja, two families on my grandfather's side. The smallest circle is Kalkatungu, which is my grandmother's side.

EARTH AND SKY

This is a memory of living on my Traditional Land
at night, laying in my swag, looking up into the night,
feeling like the stars are just there at arm's reach.
While feeling the warmth of the earth coming
through the swag, I am grounded and know
I'm at the right place at the right time.

I'm home.

MY COUNTRY

Here is a close-up of the ground that I walked over on Country while on the way to my sacred site.

MAGAJARRA (COUNTRY)

On the drive from Queensland to the Northern Territory there are a pair of hills surrounded by plains on either side of the road. They sit there overlooking the land, protecting it. We always camped at the base of one of these hills and, like the land, I always felt protected.

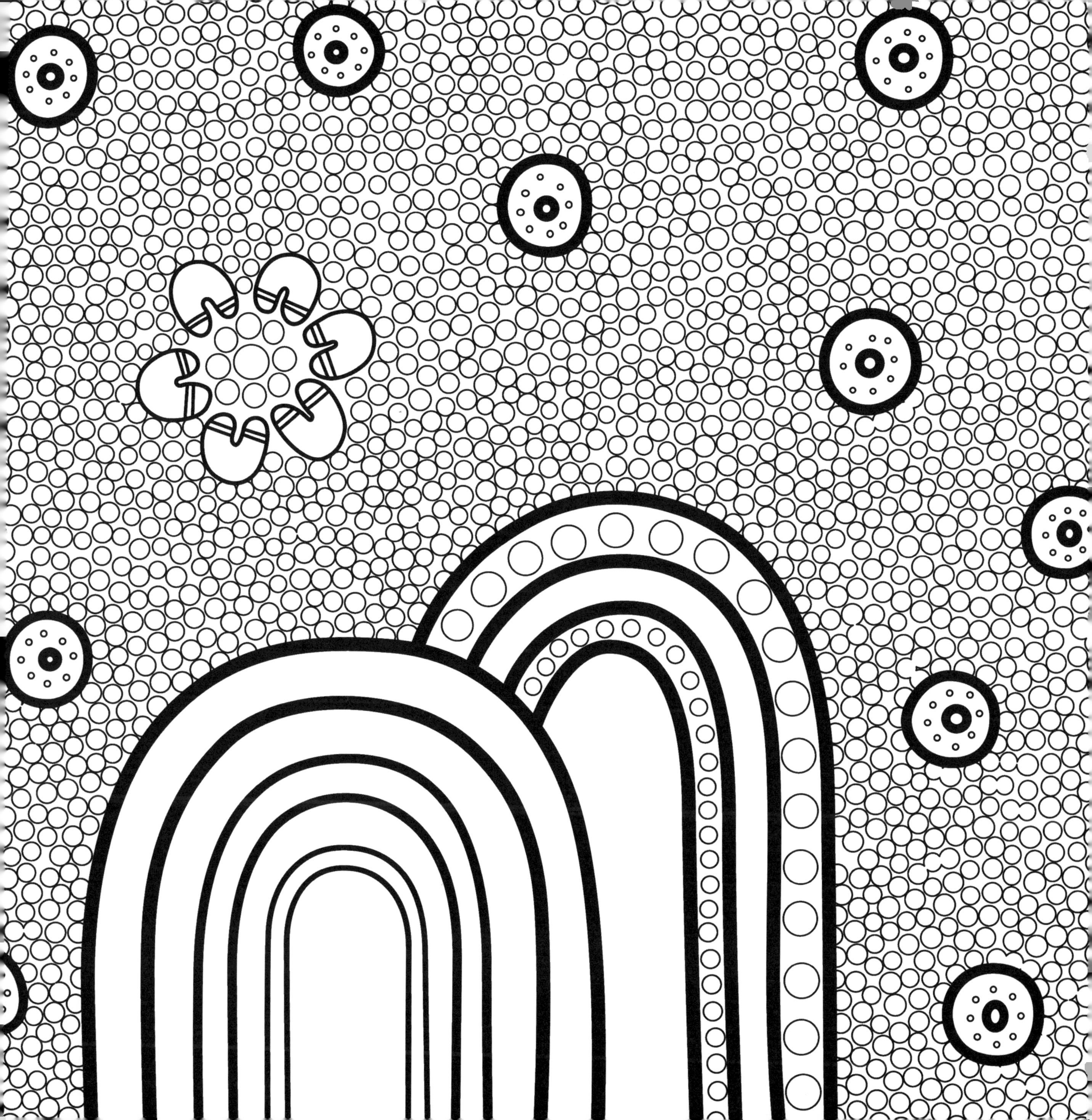

HILLS

The hills and freshwater remind me of Gudanji birth elements. In this artwork, I have covered the back landscape in spinifex to remind us that there are challenges in life.

Spinifex is a type of grass covered in wax. It rolls its leaves in on itself to hold in moisture, which creates a sharp point. My family harvest the wax and the long stalks for tool-making and ceremonial objects.

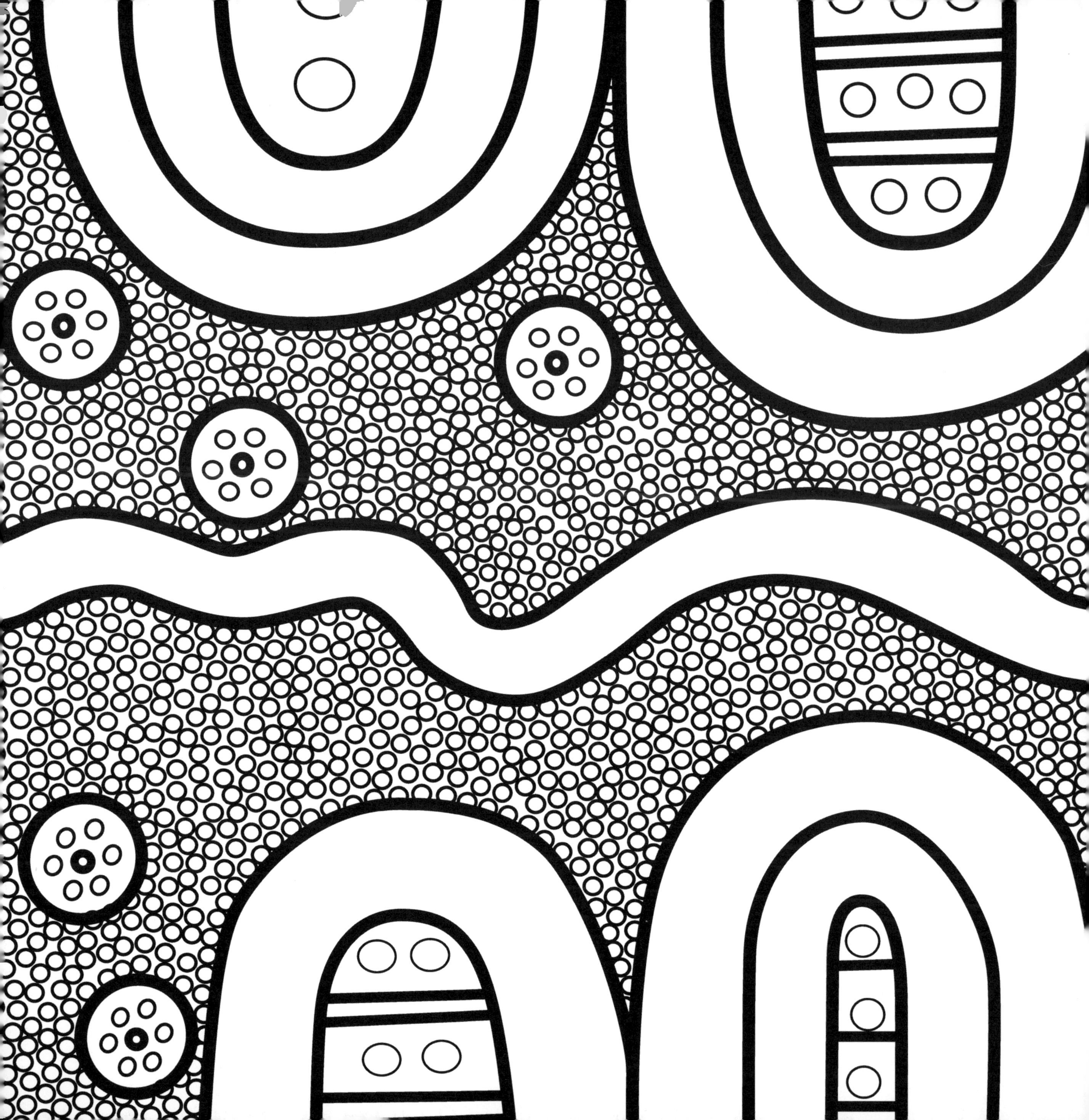

SEVEN HILLS

Artwork appears on the previous page

—

One day while out hunting, we stopped at a special place, got out of the car and walked towards a bunch of Pandanus trees. There was a natural spring in the middle of the group of trees, with little creeks running off the main waterhole. The creeks were only about 30 centimetres wide but very deep – my cousin jumped in and was instantly waist-deep. The surrounding land had spearheads and axe heads in small groups. It looked like our Old People had just got up and left.

ALIYULU (FIND)

One of my favourite memories is going out hunting for turtles. After the rain, turtles burrow under the wet ground so that when the waterhole dries up they remain in a damp environment. That's when we go out hunting using a thin hard stick. We walk in the dry waterhole bed and poke the stick into the surface, listening for the distinctive clunk on a submerged turtle's shell.

WITH FAMILY

This artwork is about searching for turtles with family. They are one of mine and my granny's favourite foods. When we go looking for long-necked turtles there is usually a whole bunch of us; we all jump into the back of the troopie and head for an almost dried-up lagoon. The water in this piece is slowly disappearing over the top of the canvas as I sit with family.

AT DUSK

A river that runs through my hometown branches into two and holds one of our main sources of food: fish. At dusk you can smell and see small campfires up and down the river – these fires are all the different families coming down to catch and cook their dinner. Kids run around together and every now and then you can hear someone playing their country music on tape.

Everyone watches out for each other because the crocodiles are also after their catch.

ONE OF MANY

This is one of many fishing spots we would go to once the rain had stopped, when all the rivers, creeks and waterholes would be flowing. On one side of the hills we would fish for barramundi and stay well away from the water where the huge saltwater crocodiles live. On the other side of the hills, we would swim in the crystal-clear fresh water and catch black bream.

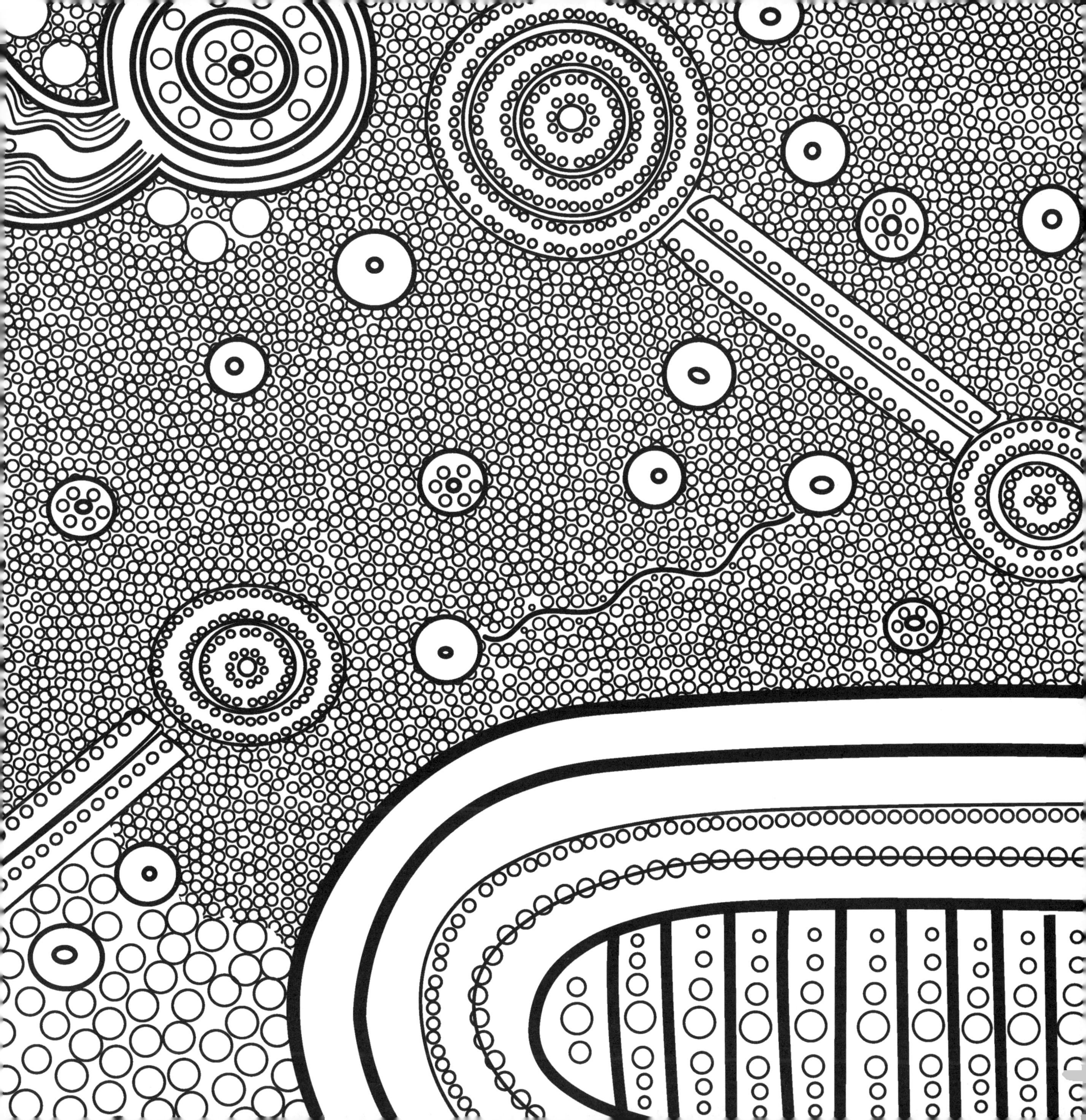

CLOSE UP

When I was eight, my Mimi (grandmother) took us to a creek on a sacred site. This artwork reminds me of the rocks at the bottom of that creek, where we swum in the crystal-clear water. I remember following the creek and finding one of the springs that fed it, where the water was coming out of the ground under a clump of spinifex. After the swim, my granny and I went fishing and caught a baby freshwater crocodile. This is one of my favourite memories.

TREK

Out bush, during dry season, we sometimes follow tracks made by cattle as they follow the rivers. These tracks are wide and clear, which make them safe to travel on.

There are many pathways made by different animals, leading to different locations.

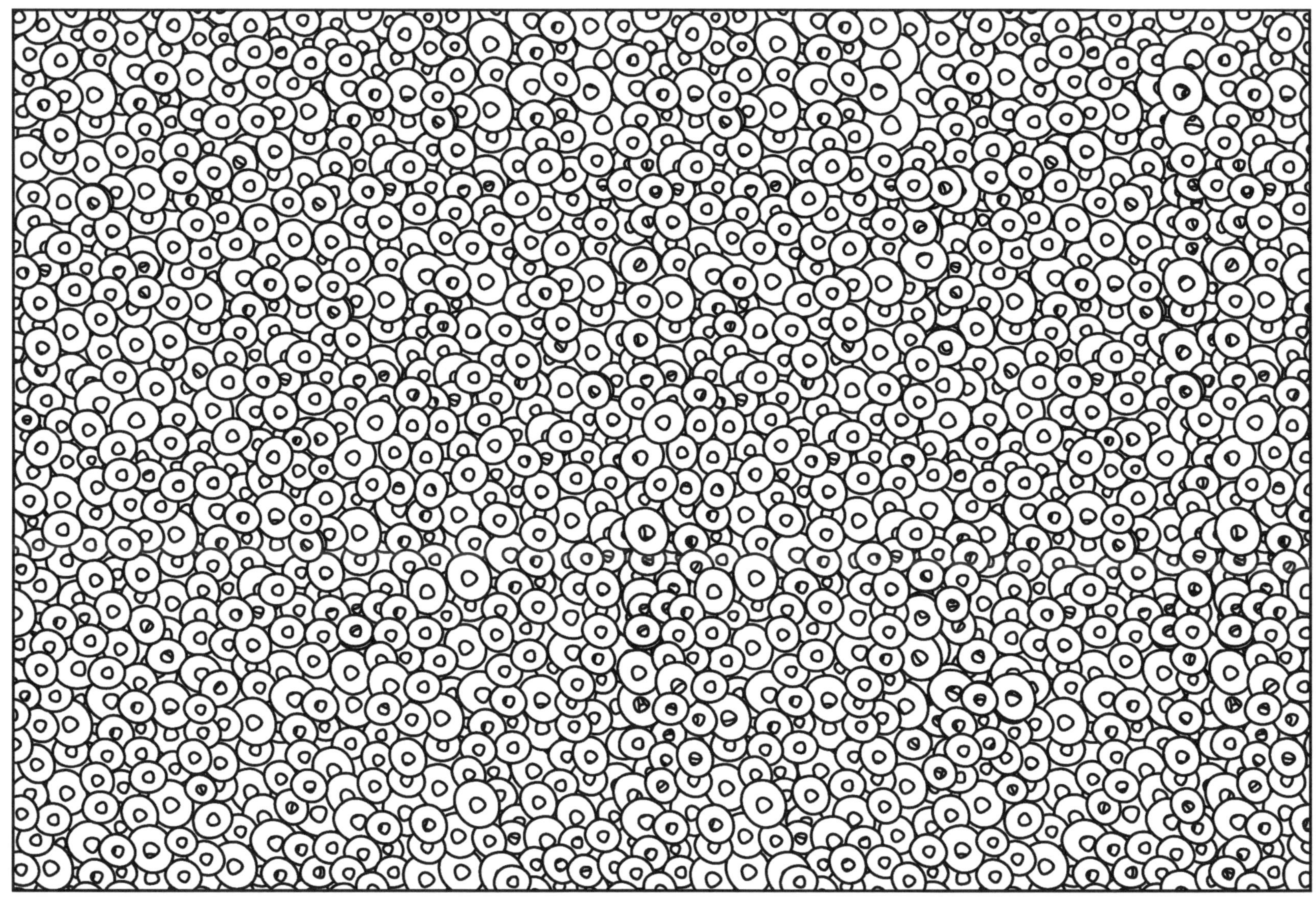

BACHELOR BUTTONS

Bachelor Buttons is about memory.

Bachelor Buttons are a type of flower – one of my mother's, sister's and my favourites, which always take us back to memories of family and Country.

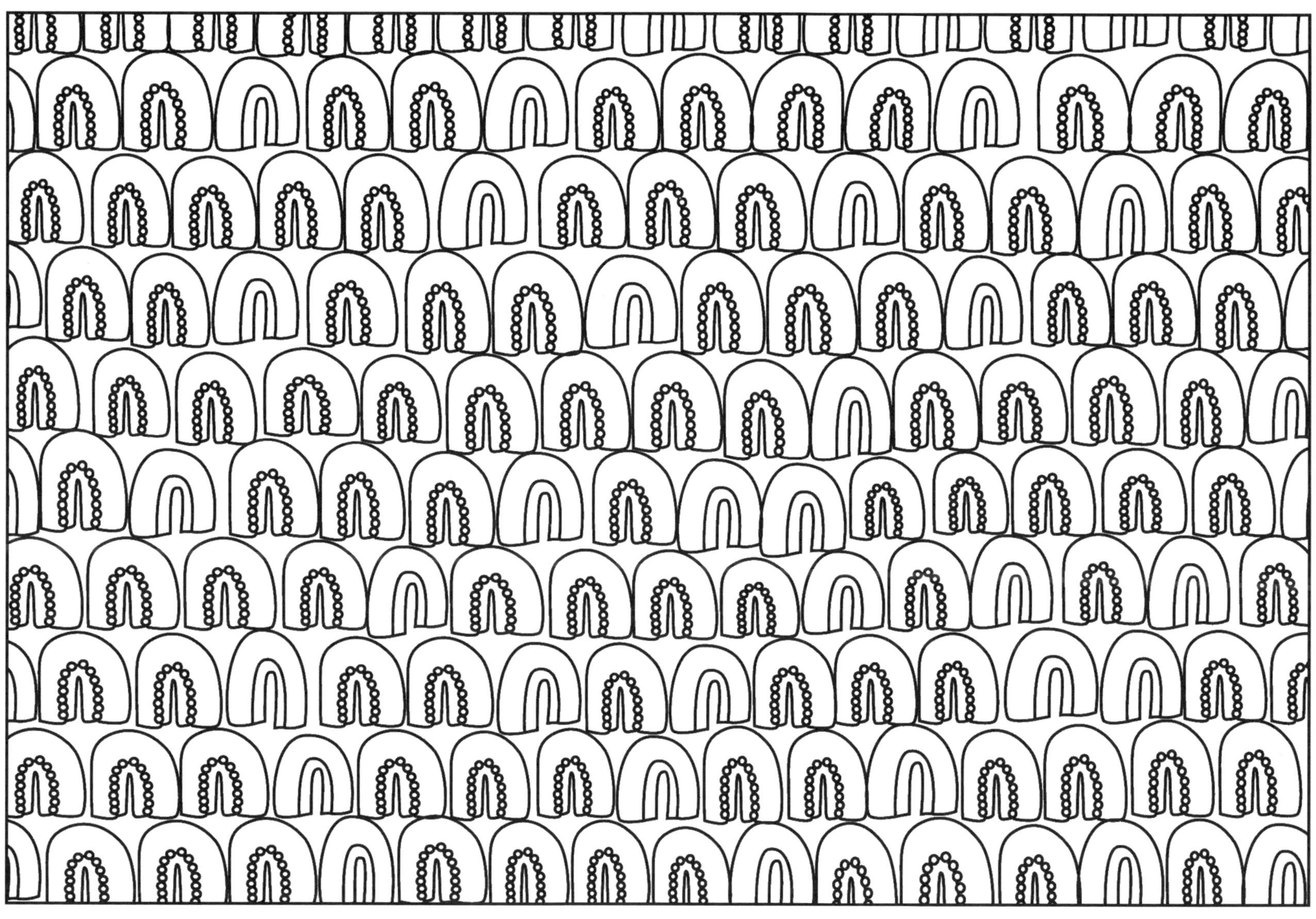

BEING

A diverse community of juwarda (people) come together, creating a strong bond and leaning on each other during testing times.

VALLEY

A family gathers around a fire in their camp eating fish they caught in the river. The land is dotted with plants and surrounded by large hills that protect them from the weather.

SURROUNDING

Camps are often positioned very deliberately: in places that have fresh water (often from a river or natural spring trickling up out of the earth), protection from the elements (usually large trees, hills or caves) and plenty of food.

BARBARRA

Barbarra is about having a safe, happy and healthy journey. It shows a journey through land, with bush plums for health and flowers for growth.

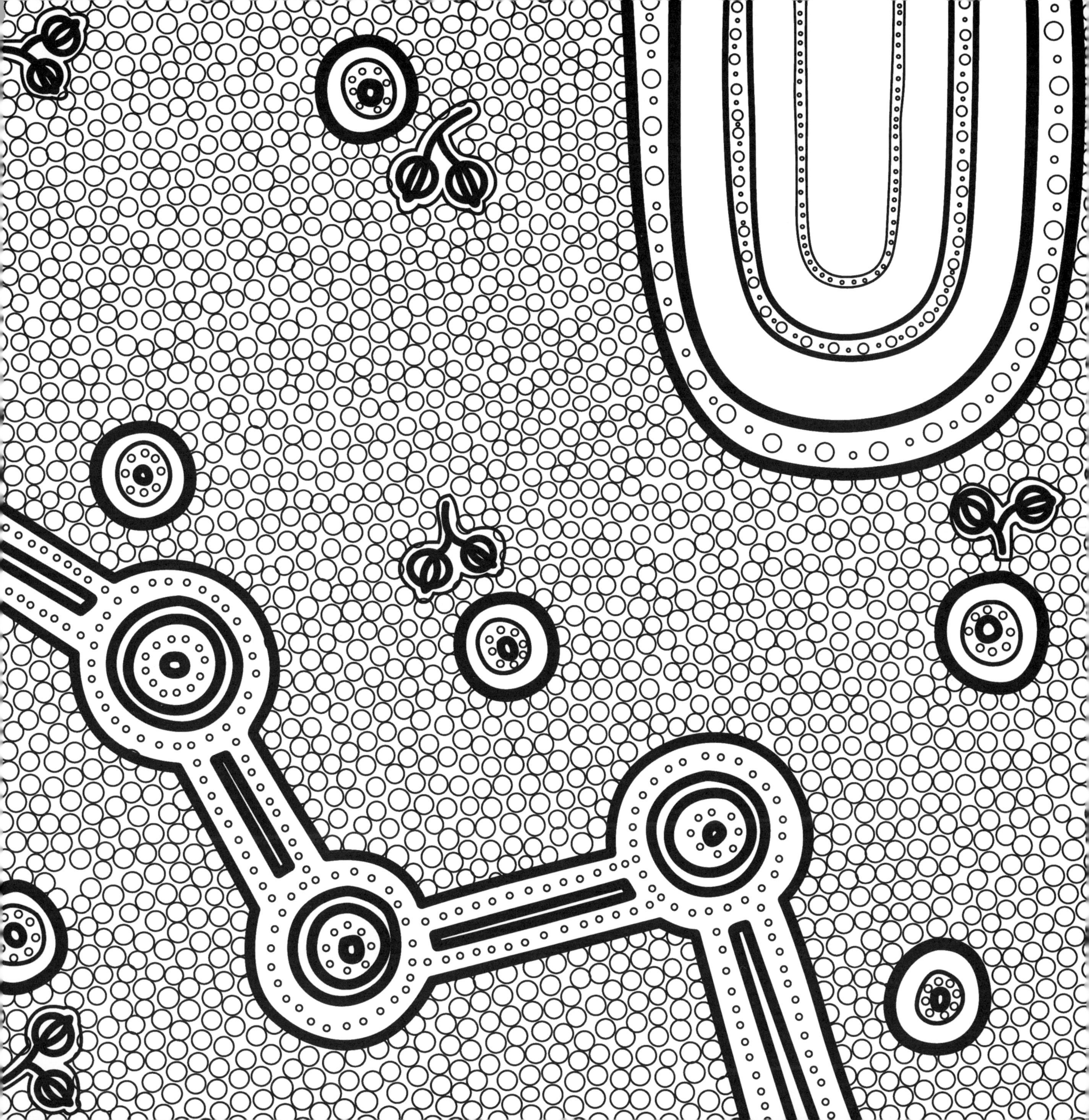

LAGIJA (SHALLOW COOLAMON)

Coolamons are used to gather food, hold items, carry hot coals and rock babies to sleep. They are made with a strong light timber and come in many different sizes. Like this artwork, they are about healing and nurturing.

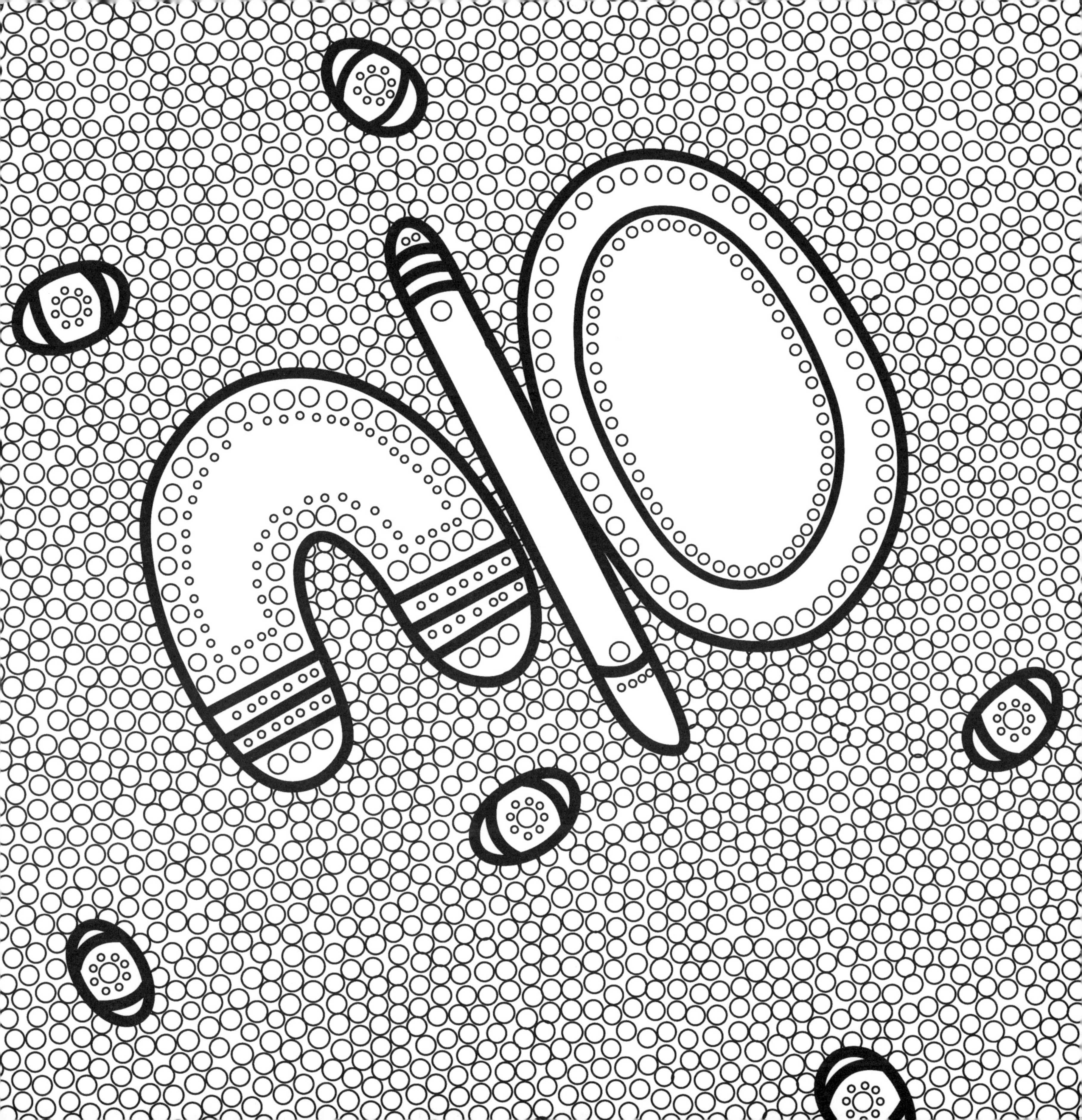

BURN OFF

This artwork is of our Country during burn-off. The land is dry and the embers are coming through, lighting small fires. The Country needs these burn-offs to regenerate.

REGENERATE

This artwork is of our Country after burning off. The extreme heat has cleared overgrown grass and bush, allowing seeds to germinate and creating new life and growth. This process is crucial for Country; an annual cycle that has provided us and our animal companions with fresh grass, vegetables, nuts and fruits for tens of thousands of years.

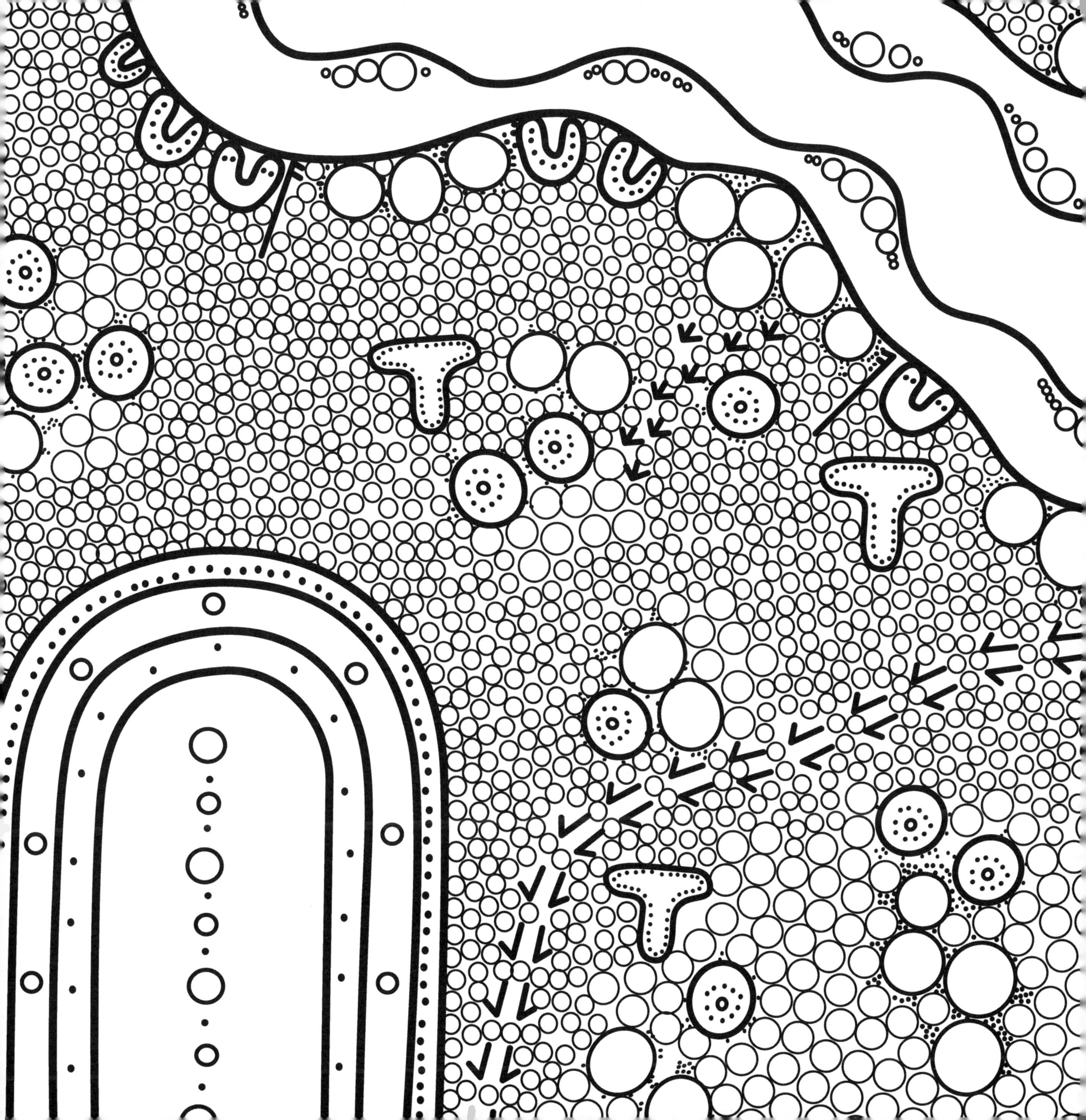

GARNUMBA (WET SEASON)

Garnumba is the wet season on Country. The creeks and rivers are flowing and the waterholes are bursting the banks. New creeks are being formed and the fish are biting.

WATERWAYS

Artwork appears on the previous page

—

In this artwork the hills and passages of connecting water bring a sense of washing away the past and bringing in fresh new life. You can see animal tracks, and people around camps and trees. A truly healthy Country.

MY MARK

Painting is my outlet. I created this because I needed to paint something. I was doing so much admin and had been on my computer for so long that I felt like I just needed to stop and make something to let my mind wander. This is what I designed.

PIECES OF ME

This is a little piece of me. It's about sitting and being quiet. Our secret sites are places to be still, to listen, to learn and to be grateful.

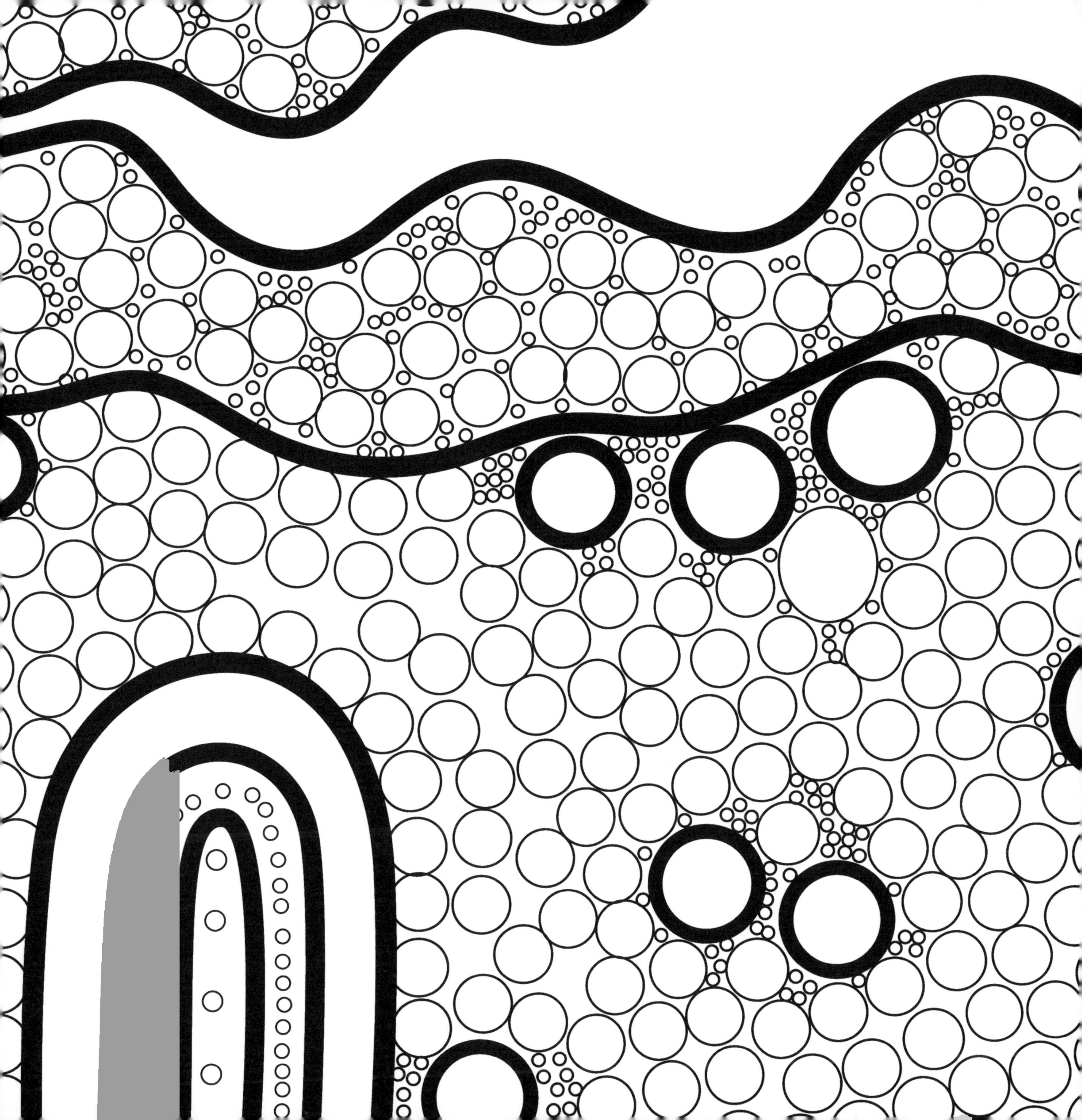

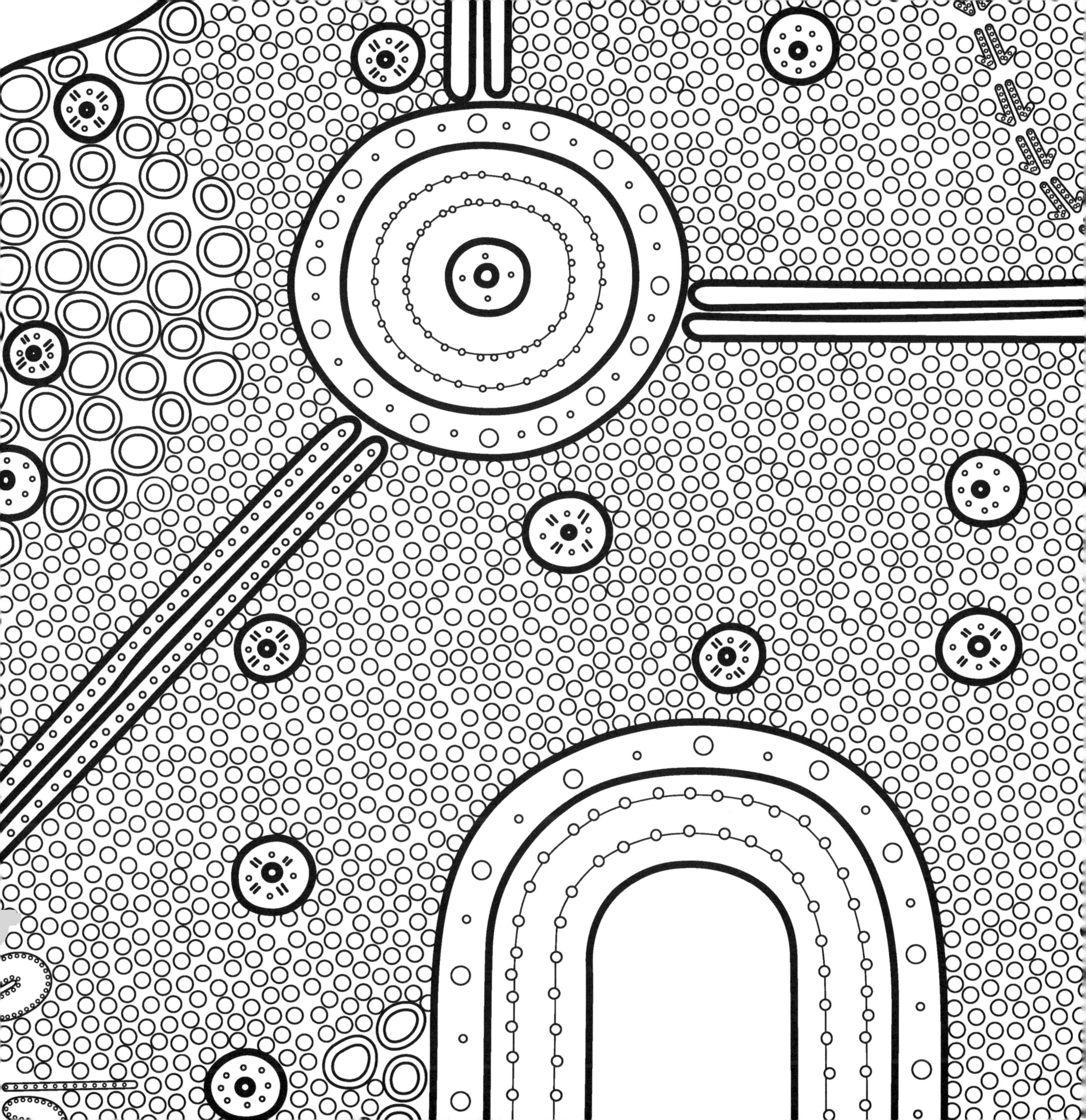

THE NEXT CHAPTER

Artwork appears on the previous page

—

The Next Chapter is about connection. It is about a couple who have travelled and shared many experiences together and are now at a time in their lives where they are focusing on their future. They have created their home and soon will be married, united as one. This couple is always surrounded by loving friends and family, supporting them in all that they do.

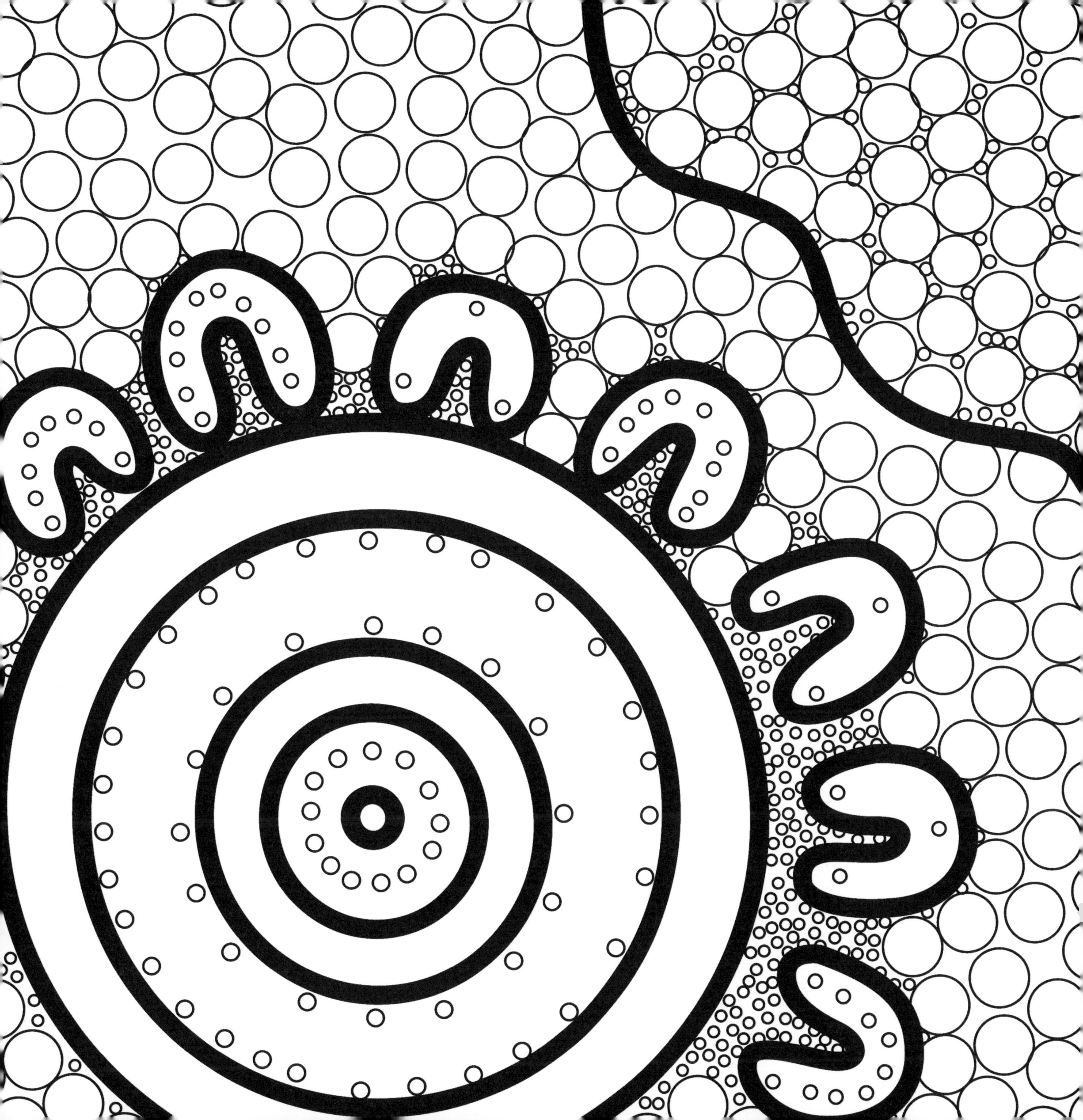

GENTLY

Tread lightly as you continue your journey, honouring and respecting the Country that surrounds you. Take moments to rest and rejuvenate, allowing the stillness of the land to seep into your soul. In this serene environment, find solace and draw inspiration from the beauty of your surroundings.

First published in Australia in 2023
by Thames & Hudson Australia Pty Ltd
11 Central Boulevard, Portside Business Park
Port Melbourne, Bunurong Country, Victoria 3207
ABN: 72 004 751 964

thamesandhudson.com.au

26 25 24 23 5 4 3 2

Thames & Hudson Australia wishes to acknowledge that Aboriginal and Torres Strait Islander people are the first storytellers of this nation and the Traditional Custodians of the land on which we live and work. We acknowledge their continuing culture and pay respect to Elders past, present and future.

ISBN 978-1-760-76411-1

A catalogue record for this book is available from the National Library of Australia

Front cover: *Solidarity,* 2021, Nardurna

Design: Casey Schuurman

Printed and bound in China by C&C Offset Printing Co., Ltd

FSC® is dedicated to the promotion of responsible forest management worldwide. This book is made of material from FSC®-certified forests and other controlled sources.

Acknowledgements

I would like to express my deepest gratitude and heartfelt appreciation to my family, your constant support and love have been the foundation of my success. Your encouragement and belief in me have propelled me forward, and I am forever grateful for your presence in my life. To my dear Mimis, your wisdom, guidance, and unconditional love have shaped me into the person I am today. Your nurturing care has been a constant source of strength and inspiration. To my beloved Country, I am humbled and honoured to call you home. I will forever love and protect you. To my partner, your unwavering love, patience, and understanding have been my foundation through every challenge and triumph. Your belief in me has been a constant source of motivation. To my incredible management, your guidance, expertise, and tireless efforts have been instrumental in shaping my professional journey. Your belief in my abilities has pushed me to new heights. Thank you all for being an integral part of my life and for your invaluable contributions to my personal and professional growth. And to my daughter Johnnie, I want to thank you for bringing immense joy and happiness into my life. You are my inspiration, and I am grateful for the love and pure happiness you bring to our family.